Dear Parent:

Congratulations! Your child is taking the first steps on an exciting journey. The destination? Independent reading!

STEP INTO READING® will help your child get there. The program offers books at five levels that accompany children from their first attempts at reading to reading success. Each step includes fun stories, fiction and nonfiction, and colorful art. There are also Step into Reading Sticker Books, Step into Reading Math Readers, and Step into Reading Phonics Readers— a complete literacy program with something to interest every child.

Learning to Read, Step by Step!

Ready to Read   Preschool–Kindergarten
• big type and easy words • rhyme and rhythm • picture clues
For children who know the alphabet and are eager to begin reading.

Reading with Help   Preschool–Grade 1
• basic vocabulary • short sentences • simple stories
For children who recognize familiar words and sound out new words with help.

Reading on Your Own   Grades 1–3
• engaging characters • easy-to-follow plots • popular topics
For children who are ready to read on their own.

Reading Paragraphs   Grades 2–3
• challenging vocabulary • short paragraphs • exciting stories
For newly independent readers who read simple sentences with confidence.

Ready for Chapters   Grades 2–4
• chapters • longer paragraphs • full-color art
For children who want to take the plunge into chapter books but still like colorful pictures.

STEP INTO READING® is designed to give every child a successful reading experience. The grade levels are only guides. Children can progress through the steps at their own speed, developing confidence in their reading, no matter what their grade.

Remember, a lifetime love of reading starts with a single step!

www.stepintoreading.com

Educators and librarians, for a variety of teaching tools, visit us at
www.randomhouse.com/teachers

Library of Congress Cataloging-in-Publication Data
Rhiannon, Ann.
Bear with me / Ann Rhiannon ; illustrated by the Disney Storybook Artists.
   p. cm. -- (Step into reading. A step 2 book)
Based on the motion picture, Brother bear, to be released in fall 2003.
Summary: When Kenai, a Native American boy living in the Pacific Northwest in prehistoric times,
is transformed into a bear, he learns about the lives of creatures other than man.
ISBN 0-7364-2174-2 -- ISBN 0-7364-8026-9 (alk. paper)
[1. Metamorphosis--Fiction. 2. Indians of North America--Northwest, Pacific--Fiction. 3.
Bears--Fiction. 4. Prehistoric animals--Fiction. 5. Human-animal relationships--Fiction. 6.
Northwest, Pacific--Fiction.] I. Disney Storybook Artists. II. Brother bear (Motion picture) III.
Title. IV. Series: Step into reading. Step 2 book.
PZ7.R343Be 2003 [E]--dc21 2003008748
Printed in the United States of America 10 9 8 7 6 5 4 3 2

STEP
2
MOVIE READER

BEAR WITH ME

By Ann Rhiannon

Illustrated by the Disney Storybook Artists

Designed by Disney's Global Design Group

Random House New York

There once was a boy
named Kenai.

One day, he turned
into a bear!

He had a tail!
And paws!
And he was
very furry.

Kenai tried to walk.

Clomp, clomp, clomp!

He tried to talk.

Growl, growl, growl!

It was hard

to be a bear!

"Please do not eat us,"
said two moose.

Kenai was confused.
"Why is everyone
afraid of me?"
he asked.

Kenai walked away—
right into a trap!
"Ouch!" he said.
Koda the bear cub
came to help.
He was not afraid
of Kenai.

Koda got Kenai
out of the trap.
"Do you want to come
to the Salmon Run?"
asked Koda.

Koda needed a friend.
Kenai needed to learn
how to be a bear.
"All right. I'll go,"
said Kenai.

They walked and walked.
Koda sang and talked.

One night,
Koda looked
at Kenai.
Then he looked up
at the sky.

"Thank you,"
Koda said.
"I have always
wanted a brother."

The next day,
they got lost.
Kenai was angry.

Koda was
angry, too.
He ran away
and hid.

Kenai looked
and looked for Koda.
He found him
by an old cave.

They saw pictures
on the walls.

Kenai saw
a picture of a man.
He missed being
a boy.
But he also liked
being a bear.

"Follow me,"
said Koda.
"I am not lost anymore."

At last,
Kenai and Koda found
the Salmon Run.

Kenai tried
to catch a fish.
Splash!

"Strange bear!"
said Tug,
the biggest bear.

Kenai felt funny.
"I do not
belong here,"
he said.

"Every bear
belongs here,"
said Tug.

Kenai tried harder
to catch a fish.
He slipped.
He swam.
He splashed.

Then he and Koda
got a big fish!

At last Kenai felt
that he belonged.

He felt like a bear.